Mia

Book 1

My New Life

Katrina Kahler

Table of Contents

The secret...

Have you ever felt that something was meant to be? That perhaps a chance meeting was not so accidental after all; almost as though it had been previously arranged and was waiting to happen.

Being in just the right place at just the right moment has to be more than coincidence. And I am convinced that Millie and I were meant to meet that day. It was as if the opportunity to cross paths had been planned all along. And when Millie accidentally bumped into me in the store, the conversation that followed seemed the most natural thing in the world.

Somehow I had known that our chance meeting would eventuate in a friendship of sorts. Call it intuition or simple gut instinct, but for some reason, I was sure we would hit it off. I also knew that a real friend was something I'd been craving my entire life.

As luck would have it, Millie herself, was in desperate need of a close friend as well. Her best friend, a girl called Julia Jones, had recently moved with her family to the country and Millie was missing her terribly. So for each of us, the timing could not have been better.

Strangely enough, I'd always been able to make friends. For me, that seemed to come easily. The problem lay in keeping them.

New kids at school were always an attraction, and I often found that I had plenty of people interested in becoming my friend and wanting to hang out with me each time I started at a new school. And believe me, this happened a lot! But the friendships never lasted. Within no time at all, they'd find me weird or strange or creepy; and then do everything they could to avoid me.

So, in time, I learned the secret was to keep my mouth shut. And when we eventually moved to Carindale and I met Millie, I instantly realized it was my opportunity to start over.

"Just don't say anything, Emmie. Keep your comments to yourself!"

They were the words I constantly repeated in my head, ones that my mom had reminded me of on so many occasions but I'd failed to listen to; which of course had resulted in the same consequences each and every time...any and all friendships I'd made were destroyed.

But when it came to Millie. I decided to finally do what I should have been doing all along.

And that was to stay quiet.

There was no way I wanted to jeopardize my chance of finally having a best friend.

That meant never, ever telling her my secret.

I also knew that if I did, my mom would make us move again. And I wanted to avoid that at all costs!

The gift...

Most people probably think that being a mind reader would be amazing. But it's far from it! Take it from one who knows...being able to read minds is definitely not at all what it's made out to be.

Mom called it a "gift." But my so-called "gift" had landed me in trouble on that many occasions, I'd lost count. The worst part was, it seemed to push people away. While it may seem cool to know what other kids are thinking, when they realized that I was constantly picking up on the thoughts in their heads, they quickly found the whole scenario very uncomfortable.

This was because I struggled to keep my reactions to myself and from a young age, I'd constantly blabbed out a comment or a question or an answer even though the other person hadn't spoken. Well, not out loud anyway.

Their looks of surprise were always the same and eventually, they'd avoid me completely. As far as they were concerned, I was creepy. And before I knew it, my status had reverted to "Loner" once again.

Or as I preferred to call it, "Loser" with a capital L.

As time passed, things gradually became worse. My mom's friends started asking questions and acting strangely around us and that was when my mom really started to worry.

"Maybe it's some kind of reaction to the trauma she's experienced," one friend suggested.

"It could be Emmie's way of trying to cope," another helpful friend added.

Then when they insisted I should be checked by a doctor or a psychologist of some sort, Mom decided we had to move, to relocate to a new town where no one knew us.

Within a matter of months, our house was sold and we were

on our way, hoping to find a nicer place filled with friendlier and more unsuspecting people. And that had been the beginning of the pattern that followed.

Rather than trying to deal with each situation, my mom's choice was always to run away. And because she owned an online business, she was able to work anywhere that had an Internet connection.

"Let's just leave, Em! The kids at that school aren't nice anyway. We'll move somewhere else. We'll rent a nice new house and you can go to another school where you can make real friends."

Deep down, I knew that she was scared; terrified that someone might learn the truth about her mind-reading daughter. She was convinced if that happened, I'd be in danger of being abducted by some government agency or foreign power, and then I'd be put under lock and key while they conducted ongoing extensive scientific experiments to determine how my brain worked.

It all seemed a bit far-fetched to me, but she was sure that something terrible would happen and she'd never see me again. So, almost daily, she reminded me of the urgent need to stay quiet about what I was capable of doing.

"You have a gift, Emmie. But it has to be our secret. Ours and ours alone. If anyone finds out, then we will be torn apart. I know it!"

At least my 'lack of friends' problem made relocating easier. Well, much easier than it would have been if I were a normal, everyday kind of person, I guess; one who didn't have hidden powers that made everyone around her feel uneasy. Although I had to admit, moving house every six to twelve months or so, certainly was over-kill.

This time, however, I was determined to make it work. It was the summer holidays and I had Millie to hang out with. And in addition to having a real friend, one who did not find me creepy and strange, I also soon discovered that she had some pretty cool friends of her own.

There were a couple of boys in particular who had caught my eye, and for a change, it seemed that I finally had something to look forward to!

How it all began...

One of my earliest memories is of my 4th birthday. At that time, my dad was still alive and although the memory is vague in parts, it's something I am particularly grateful for because it is one of the few memories I have of my dad.

My mother had made a beautiful cake that she'd covered in decorative flower shapes made from delicious pink icing. It was the prettiest cake I had ever seen.

Sitting excitedly on my dad's lap, I watched Mom light the candles one by one, mesmerized by the sparkling glow in front of me. Then, after waiting patiently for my parents to sing happy birthday, I attempted to blow out each of the four little flames. But they were quite stubborn and continued to remain lit. All the while, the room was filled with happy laughter at my feeble attempts.

It finally took Mom's help and all four flames disappeared. But when I looked into her eyes, instead of the joy that had been there only moments earlier, all I could see was terrible sadness.

"What's wrong with Daddy?" I gasped, turning abruptly towards the face of the man who held me on his lap. "Is he really going to die?"

I'd heard my parents comment before...that I seemed older than my years; that I seemed to know things that I shouldn't, that I was too smart for my own good.
But their reaction in that moment was more of an intense shock than a surprise.

The instant the words had left my lips, the look of horror

that appeared on my mother's face, said it all. I'd found out their secret. The one they'd attempted to hide from me, and try as she might to distract me, it was no use. I ran hysterically to my room; the melted blobs of wax sitting in a thick lumpy layer on top of the icing on the cake that I had been in awe of only minutes before.

I remember feeling so scared that I tried to hide in the corner, clutching tightly to the teddy that I had been given at birth and which so many years later, I still kept in a prime position on top of the pillows on my bed.

My father was going to die. I had heard my mother's voice in my head and although I struggled to understand where that voice had come from, I knew what I had heard. And I also knew what death was.

Earlier that year, the puppy my dad had brought home unexpectedly, had been hit by a car and killed. In the short time we had owned that puppy, I'd become so attached that I was heartbroken when he died. And in the process, I learned that death was a permanent thing, causing something or someone you love to disappear and never return. I was terrified that this was going to happen to my father.

My 4th birthday had been the first real sign of my "gift". Sometime later, there was another occasion when once again, I knew exactly what my parents were thinking. I could distinctly hear their voices in my head and it was as though they were speaking directly to me. But when I glanced in their direction, they were sitting at the kitchen table not saying a word.

I replied anyway and I remember my mom laughing and jokingly calling me her little "mind reader". But rather than being amused, my dad simply frowned and told me I was imagining things.

He hadn't fooled me though. Even at that young age, I knew I had heard their thoughts; the voices were real and not imaginary. And I was also aware that it was not normal to be a "mind reader".

Then, sure enough, it was only a matter of months before my father's illness became obvious and his condition rapidly began to decline. He only lasted another year and then the terminal blood disease that had been making him so ill took his life. After that, my mom and I were left on our own.

I didn't have too many memories of my dad, but I could feel his presence around me. Sometimes it was stronger than others and I knew that he was there. It was a comforting feeling and helped me to cope with all the problems I had to face in the years after he died.

Being constantly labeled as weird, strange or creepy was no fun at all. Sometimes I tried to laugh it off, but deep down inside, it hurt more than anything.

While I attempted to ignore the taunts from the other kids, I could not escape their voices in my head. Even though some were too polite to say the words, "You're a freak" to my face, I knew exactly what they were thinking. I could hear their thoughts as clearly as if they'd spoken them.

And every time Mom and I tried our luck in a new town, the scene was repeated all over again.

Questions...

One Saturday morning, several years after my father's death, I sat alone in my room with my favorite teddy for company and I recalled the day my father passed away. Overwhelmed with sadness at the time, I had taken little notice of the tingling sensation that passed through my body as I held his hand. Sitting at the side of his hospital bed while the machines beeped noisily at his side, I was aware of very little except the faint sound of his breathing.

But for some reason, that morning so many years later, I remembered the strange feeling distinctly. It was kind of a buzzing tingle underneath my skin and it had seemed to work its way into my fingers as my dad took his last breath. The memory became so vivid that I could almost feel that exact sensation once again. It was as though the mysterious power that I'd been gifted with had been transferred in its full intensity from him to me the moment he died.

While there had been a couple of times in my younger years when I'd been able to hear voices in my head, my parents had dismissed my remarks and the situation appeared to be forgotten.

Ever since that tragic day however, I was aware that something unusual was going on and the voices became a much more regular occurrence. It was as if my ability to read minds grew stronger with each passing year. So much so, I eventually had to ask the question that had been worrying me for quite some time.

"Mom, was Dad a mind reader too? Could he read minds like me?"

She looked curiously towards me, a concerned frown appearing on her face as she considered the possibility. I could see that she was tossing the idea around in her head and she was very quiet for a moment, obviously deep in thought over my suggestion.

Her expression gradually changed and I watched carefully as she came to terms with what she had obviously tried to ignore for so long.

Shaking her head in confusion, she replied. "I don't know, Emmie. But if your father could do what you are now capable of, surely I would have known about it. And besides, he confided in me all the time. If he could read minds, don't you think he would have told me?"

She doesn't believe me!

Although Mom tried to deny it, I was convinced that my dad had the "gift" too. I could think of no other explanation. Almost certainly, I must have inherited it from someone. And something deep inside told me that he had been a mind reader as well.

Moving house did nothing for my curiosity though. I still wanted answers. If my dad really was a mind reader, why had he kept it a secret? Why would he not share that detail with Mom? And surely he realized before he died that I'd shown signs of being a mind reader like him.

There were too many questions that I did not know the answers to. I knew there must be an explanation and I was desperate to find it.

Meanwhile, the challenge lay in keeping my secret safe, the way my dad had done. No one could know except Mom and me.

It was up to me to stay quiet and keep all my thoughts and remarks silent. But going by my past record, I wasn't sure if that were possible.

Carindale...

As it turned out, moving to Carindale was the best thing we could have done. We managed to rent a lovely house that was situated only a short distance from the mall; this suited me perfectly because I loved hanging out at the shops and looking for clothes. Ever since my 12th birthday, Mom had given me permission to go to the shops on my own. Not that I was able to buy too much as she only gave me a small allowance. But it was better than always sitting at home on my computer watching YouTube videos or repeats of my favorite television series.

Although my mother worked from home and was usually around, most of the time she was busy working. So she often encouraged me to invite friends over, or at least she attempted to. But whenever I did, the answer was always the same.

"Sorry, I'm busy."

I knew that was a lie though. Their excuses did not fool me. As well as the words they spoke, I also heard the voices in their heads. And I was fully aware of what my 'friends' were really thinking. Sometimes their thoughts were so mean, I'd have to catch my breath.

"OMG! No way!"

"Haha! What a joke! As if I'd give up my weekend to hang out with you."

"You're so weird. There's no way I want to go to your house!"

I would always struggle to prevent the tears that threatened to drip into full view onto my reddened cheeks.

If only I didn't know their true thoughts, at least that way I'd be spared the embarrassment and the humiliation. It was just too upsetting and I could not bear to put myself through it any longer. So in the end, I decided to avoid trying to make friends altogether. It just wasn't worth it.

Until I met Millie that was.

And then, as if by magic, everything changed!

Unexpected excitement...

It was only a few days after Millie and I had first met that I received her text. Being the summer holidays, she was looking for things to do and when she asked if I wanted to hang out at the mall, I could literally feel my excitement bubbling over.

But the moment I replied, I realized I had a problem. Quickly scanning my wardrobe, I searched for something to wear. This was the most important event of my entire life and I couldn't see anything that I was at all interested in changing into. There was no way I could turn up to meet Millie in the old jeans and T-shirt that I'd put on that morning. The situation was a disaster and I could feel a rush of anxiety settling in the pit of my stomach.

I was sure that Millie would be wearing something really nice. Her gorgeous outfit had been the first thing I'd noticed as soon as we bumped into each other. And I was sure that her entire wardrobe was filled with clothes just as pretty.

Thinking back to my mom's invitation to go shopping just the day before, I shook my head in frustration. She'd suggested we go on a bit of a spending spree to celebrate our latest move. But for some stupid reason, I'd decided to postpone the idea until the weekend. Obviously though, if I hadn't made that silly mistake I wouldn't be facing the problem I'd found myself in.

Even though I knew I was to blame, I burst into her office to complain about my lack of clothes. I had to complain to someone and she was always the one forced to deal with my outbursts. But as soon as I'd finished ranting about how bad my clothing situation was, without a word whatsoever, she turned to her cupboard and pulled out the perfect solution.

In her hands, she held up a very pretty blue and white striped top, one that I'd never seen before but was obviously meant for me. It was almost like a magic act where the magician pulled a rabbit out of a hat and the children gasped with delight. For me, the reaction was exactly the same and I could feel a beaming smile quickly spread across my face. She then explained that she'd bought it as a surprise and when she asked if I'd like to wear it that day, I instantly threw my arms around her neck in a grateful hug.

"Oh Mom, you're a life saver. Thank you so much!! It will go perfectly with my black shorts."

When I looked at my reflection in the bedroom mirror a few minutes later, I was more than happy with the result. I absolutely loved the top and felt so thankful to have been given it.

But then my gaze took in the whole image of the person staring back; big brown eyes, freckles dotted across my nose and cheeks and long brown hair, slightly wavy and in need of a good trim.

I didn't mind my face and hair so much but it was the long skinny legs hanging out the bottom of my shorts that really bothered me. I'd always been tall and lanky, and regardless of the huge amounts of food that I ate, I struggled to put on weight.

"You can eat anything, Emmie. You're so lucky! You could be a fashion model one day."

My mother's words rang in my head when I thought of her amazed reaction each night as she watched me demolish platefuls of food. But her remarks did little to improve my own opinion of the way I looked. I was embarrassed, simple as that! So embarrassed in fact, that I'd even make excuses to avoid swimming in public. Especially if there happened to be lots of other kids around.

When I was younger, it was never an issue. I had always loved swimming and it was also something that I was quite good at. But at my first school swimming carnival a few years earlier, I noticed a lot of kids staring in my direction. At first, I thought they were surprised to see me win so many races and also that they were impressed by the number of ribbons I'd won.

But when I tuned into their thoughts, I found that what they were really thinking was very different to anything I could ever have imagined.

"Wow! She's so skinny!"

"Haha! Check out that girl. She's like a bean pole."

"OMG. That girl looks so bad. I'd hate to be that thin!"

Horrified at what I'd heard, I quickly threw my towel around my shoulders and raced to the bathroom to change. From that moment on, I pretended to be feeling unwell and refused to swim in any more races. All I wanted was to be left on my own in misery, away from the stares of the other kids.

Even though the teachers tried to encourage me to continue, there was no way that I could be coaxed back into the water. And when another girl was awarded the age champion medal instead of me, I didn't care. No medal was worth the humiliation of kids staring at me the way they had done.

What hurt the most, however, was the mean, ugly thoughts that had filled their heads.

That was the beginning of my body conscious behavior. At least that's what my mom called it and in an effort to help, she would double the quantities of food in my lunch box each day and offer extra helpings for dinner. But regardless of how much I ate, I could not put on weight. Gradually I grew taller, but this only made me look lankier than ever.

Occasionally, I'd catch my mom watching me, her eyes filled with worried concern.

And I knew exactly what she was thinking.

"Emmie is so beautiful. Why can't she see it?"

But my mother's thoughts were very different to my own and I scoffed at the remarks racing through her head.

As I stood staring at my reflection that morning, I prayed for the hundredth time that my body would improve as I grew older.

Then, with the sudden realization that I was going to be late if I didn't hurry, I was forced to turn away from the vision in the mirror and quickly race out of my room. As I did, I happened to notice the photo that was taken of my dad and myself when I was little, and I instantly felt a familiar calming sensation take hold. It seemed that he always appeared when I needed him most and for that, I was truly thankful.

Brushing away all anxious thoughts, I headed quickly for the front door, a growing sense of excitement causing the smile to return to my face. After giving my mom another brief hug of thanks for the beautiful top that I was so grateful to have been given, I waved goodbye before disappearing from sight.

Right then, I forced all negative thoughts out of my head, choosing instead to focus on the image of the friendly girl waiting to meet me.

However, I was completely unaware of what was in store for me that day. Nor did I have any idea of the new power I would soon be capable of.

This discovery would be the beginning of some unforeseen events. And right then, if anyone had tried to warn me, I would not have believed them.

The discovery...

Sitting in the booth of a burger bar a few hours later, Millie and I continued to laugh and chat as we munched on the food in front of us. We seemed to have so much in common and several of Millie's favorite things were exactly the same as my own; the same food, the same songs and even the same movies. Although we'd only known each other for a short time, it was so easy to hang out with her, almost as if we'd been friends forever. I was also aware that she felt exactly the same way about me.

I'd made sure not to comment or give any indication I knew what she was thinking, but it was great to know that I'd finally made a real friend. Right then I was the happiest girl alive.

As we sat eating our lunch, an idea appeared abruptly in my mind. I had no clue at all as to where it had come from, but I knew instinctively that it was the key. I had to control my powers. If I didn't, my life would continue to be a misery and that was something I definitely wanted to avoid. I was also prepared to try anything in order not to ruin the friendship that was forming between Millie and myself.

For me to read minds, all I had to do was concentrate on a person's thoughts. But why not reverse that power and focus on blocking them instead?

The idea seemed so simple, I couldn't understand why I hadn't thought of it before. However, the only way I'd know if it would work was to give it a try. And I decided that right then was as good a time as any.

Millie was in the middle of telling me about the band she'd formed the year before with her friends, Julia, Blake, and Jack and I was amazed to hear that she had actually been the lead singer. It sounded such a cool thing to do and I tried my best to listen carefully to every detail.

At the same time, I began to build an invisible brick wall in my mind. Although it took a huge amount of effort to concentrate on the two tasks at once, I found that if I focused hard enough, it was possible to listen to Millie's conversation and create the wall as well.

Obviously, the wall didn't really exist, it was just a figment of my imagination, kind of like an invisible barrier inside my head. But instead of blocking Millie's face from view, all it blocked were her thoughts. And as the seconds ticked by, I realized that with each brick added, the weaker my power became. Until, at last, all I could hear was the sound of the words coming directly from Millie's moving lips. The thoughts in her head remained hers and hers alone.

For me, this discovery seemed a miracle of huge proportions. It was a serious breakthrough and although it needed intense concentration, it was definitely worth the effort.

Up until then, I'd spent most of my time pushing people away; simply because they found me too weird. But I was sure that if I could master this skill then my problems would be over.

When Millie hopped up to find the bathroom, I decided to test my discovery on the man sitting in the booth next to ours. He was facing my way and the perfect target to practice on. But before I had a chance to start, his thoughts unexpectedly found their way inside my mind; passing through as clearly as if he were sitting right next to me.

"I reckon I can grab that wallet. Probably the phone too. That stupid girl is so busy talking, she won't even notice."

Paying closer attention, I began to concentrate more intensely. I also took in his unusual appearance. Even though it was the middle of summer, he had the collar of his long sleeved coat standing up stiffly around his neck. And his unshaven face reminded me of a sinister cartoon type character; the typical stereotype of a robber or thief and I wondered briefly if all thieves tended to look that way. His hair was greasy and unwashed and he had smears of dirt across his cheeks. I guessed he might be a homeless person of some sort, but I could not feel sorry for him, not after realizing what he was up to.

His eyes darted back and forth towards the table across the aisle from mine, where I could see a group of teenage girls deep in conversation. And on the very edge was sitting the wallet that he was planning to steal. At the same time, the girls were so engrossed in each other, they were unaware of anything going on around them.

"This'll be easy! All I've got to do is grab it as I go past."

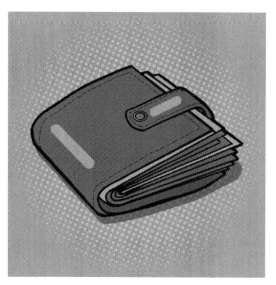

The voice in my head was more of a snarl and I could feel my skin crawl at the sound of it. But he must have felt me watching him because his gaze abruptly turned towards me.

Like a cornered rat, he seemed alert to everything going on around him and with a start, I wondered for a moment if he was picking up on what I was thinking. It was a disturbing thought but I forced myself to brush it away. I knew that if I didn't act fast, it would be too late. At the same time though, I didn't want to draw attention to myself. However, I could think of no other option.

Without stopping to consider the consequences, I stood up as if to head towards the front counter, but when I stepped into the aisle, I pretended to stumble over an unseen object on the floor. Grabbing hold of the girls' table for support, I nudged the wallet and phone away from the edge.

Instantly, the entire group of girls looked at me with concern, asking if I were okay. While they were all distracted, I discreetly pushed the objects further into the middle of the table. Then, turning back to my seat, I sat back down in my original spot. The girl sitting closest gave me an odd look, but in the spur of the moment it had been all I could think of; apart from declaring to the entire café that the dirty looking man sitting opposite was a thief.

Unfortunately, he had watched my every move and when I looked his way, our eyes locked in place. His intense stare was full of disgust and all I could do was stare guiltily back.

I could hear every word, every thought that filled his head and my stomach churned at the foul language he was directing towards me. But I kept my eyes fixed on him, even though his evil glare was causing the hairs on my arms to stand on end.

Without warning, he was on his feet, moving with the

stealth of a prowling animal, hunting its prey. The items he'd intended to steal were beyond his reach but he paused beside me and scowled angrily while I sat deathly still in my place. Too scared to move, all I could do was stare back and hope that he would keep walking.

"Don't ever do that again!"

This time he spoke aloud and then he was gone.

With a quick glance behind me, I caught sight of his distinct figure as he made his way through the crowd just outside the café. And with my pulse racing, I smiled weakly at Millie who had just slid back into her seat opposite mine.

"Are you feeling okay?" she asked with a frown. "You look really pale."

"I think I just need some fresh air," I replied, taking a deep breath.

Following along close behind her as we made our way to the nearby exit of the shopping complex, I scanned the area anxiously hoping that the man was nowhere in sight.

He was one person I did not want to meet again and I struggled to shake away the scene I had just left behind.

What worried me most though, was the uneasy feeling that remained in the pit of my stomach and I looked quickly around, almost sure that I could feel him watching me.

Later that night as I lay in bed, tossing and turning and unable to sleep, I replayed the event over in my head.

While I was grateful to be able to help the girl, even though she had no idea of how close she had been to her things being stolen, I knew it was an experience I could have done without.

For me, reading people's minds constantly led to problems and I was still feeling very uneasy about what had happened that afternoon.

I knew that my mom called my mind reading ability a gift and said I should put it to good use, but all it seemed to do was get me into trouble. I'd had enough. I really could not deal with it any longer. And I decided right then that I must do what I could to make my life easier. I'd discovered a way to block any and all thoughts around me and I must find a way to practice that skill so it became a habit.

I also knew that it was up to me to make that happen.

New friends...

Millie and I had begun to hang out regularly. She was definitely the funniest and nicest girl I had ever met and I constantly found myself in hysterics over her random comments. If she was busy doing other things and we couldn't catch up then we'd simply text or direct message each other on Instagram.

My mom had bought me a mobile phone for my 12th birthday but I'd never used it much before, as I had no friends to contact. Since meeting Millie though, it was constantly making a pinging sound as we texted each other back and forth.

I was extremely grateful to have made such a nice friend but there was just one problem. As the days went by, something that didn't bother me at first, gradually became more and more of an issue. While I realized I should not be complaining, I found it hard to ignore.

Try as I might, I could not come to terms with Millie's constant chatter about her friend, Julia. It seemed that she was always being reminded of her and in just about every conversation, she mentioned her name.

"Julia loves doing that."

"Julia is so funny! She always cracks me up."

"I wish Julia were here so I could ask her opinion."

"Julia and I have been best friends for so long! I can't believe she doesn't live here anymore!"

"Julia, Julia, Julia…"

While I understood that they were very close and Millie was still getting used to not having her around, the fact that she could not stop talking about her had become a little annoying and more than a little upsetting.

Although Millie and I had only recently met, I desperately wanted her to think of me as her bestie. An actual close friend who I could tell all my secrets to was something I'd never had. While I knew there was one secret I could never share, I still wanted someone who thought of me as their best friend. However, when she invited me to her house one day, I was able to see first-hand how close she and Julia actually were.

On her bedroom shelves sat a heap of pretty photo frames and most of them contained pics of the two girls together. In each and every one, they both wore a beaming smile and it was obvious how much fun they'd had when they were together. While I couldn't help but feel a little envious, I began to understand how difficult it must have been for Millie when Julia had left. It also made me wonder how Julia was coping without Millie.

There was a great shot of the two of them sitting side by side on the front step of a house. Julia had her arm draped loosely around Millie's shoulder and the pair seemed completely content. With her head tilted and her eyes crinkled with amusement, Julia gazed into the distance. Millie was looking at Julia and laughing happily. The pair were obviously enjoying a funny moment together, their pose completely natural as they focused on each other and whatever it was they had shared, the two of them completely unaware of the camera.

Julia's big brown eyes and long dark hair were set off

beautifully by the pretty pink top she was wearing, while Millie's blue T-shirt contrasted with it perfectly. It really was a gorgeous photo and gave a true impression of how close they were.

Another picture showed the two of them dressed up in really cool Halloween outfits. They both looked amazing and I thought about how much fun that night must have been.

As I continued to scan the frames, stopping to admire each photo individually, my eyes fell upon one that immediately caught my interest. Rather than just the two girls, there were a couple of boys in the shot as well. One of them wore a cheeky grin while the other was making a funny face as he stared into the camera. I took in every detail of that photo, especially the close friendship amongst them. I then tried picturing myself as part of that group with my own face taking the place of Julia's.

"This is such a great shot, Millie." I smiled admiringly as I looked towards her. "Are these the boys in your band?"

"Yes they are!" she exclaimed, as she jumped up from her place on the bed. "Good guess, Em. That one is Blake and the one with the silly expression is Jack. He's always joking around!"

"It's such a cool photo," I replied. "And they're both so good looking!"

She laughed in response. "Yeah, I used to think so too. Well, I still think that Blake is. But he's Julia's boyfriend," she added before continuing. "I used to have a huge crush on Jack but that was a long time ago. We're just friends now."

"Wow!" I exclaimed with interest. "I can see why you liked him. He's really cute."

Millie grinned before replying. "There's another boy I had a crush on before school ended. I was hoping to bump into him over the summer, but so far I haven't seen him around at all. His name's Alec. And he's *really* good looking!"

Laughing in response, I could not help my next comment, "So many good looking boys in Carindale, Millie!"

And then, as I stared more closely at the photo, another

thought occurred to me, "Poor Julia! She must really miss Blake!"

I was finding it hard to understand how she could leave someone like that behind. But then, as Millie had already told me, she had no choice. Her dad was starting a new job and they all had to move whether they wanted to or not.

"Yeah, she misses him heaps," Millie agreed, "But they call each other almost every night. So I guess that helps."

Staring more intently at the photo, Millie recalled the day it was taken. "That was when we all went to the local theme park. I think it was one of the best days I've ever had!"

I watched her as she focused on her memories. Then, without warning her smile abruptly disappeared, and for a moment I felt sure she was going to cry. When she turned her back on me, I searched for something to say; anything to help her feel better.

"Maybe we could do something fun together, Millie? And maybe you could even introduce me to some of your friends. I'd love to meet them."

I held the group photo in my hand and hoped she'd pick up on the hint I was trying to make. Then, turning to me with a smile, I could see her eyes brighten.

"I'll give Blake a call tonight and see what they're up to," she replied eagerly, all traces of sadness disappearing from her face. "That would be a lot of fun, Em and I'm sure you'll like them!"

"Sounds great," I replied happily, and at the same time, I tried to contain the excitement I felt bubbling inside.

I didn't want to appear too enthusiastic about the idea of meeting Blake and Jack but it seemed that things were heading in the right direction. For me, having a group of cool people to hang out with would be a dream come true and although Millie missed Julia terribly, I knew that we were gradually becoming good friends. It would probably take some time, but that was okay. I would just have to be patient.

Later that night when I was in bed and trying to sleep, I realized something else had also taken place during my visit to Millie's. For the first time since we started hanging out together, I had not read her thoughts, not even once. Although tempted at one stage, I controlled myself and focused on building a wall in my mind instead.

It was something I'd been practicing on my mom and was gradually becoming better at. I could also see that each time I practiced, it became quicker and easier than the time before. Hopefully soon, it would be automatic. That was what I needed to aim for.

As I replayed the events of the day, I also recalled the group photo I'd spent so much time admiring, and once again, a flutter of excitement took hold in my stomach. To be part of a group, just hanging out and having fun, especially with Millie and the two boys in that picture, was definitely something to look forward to.

With that thought foremost in my mind, I finally drifted into a deep sleep. And when I woke the next morning, I was sure that my smile from the night before was still fixed firmly in place. The feeling of excitement was quite new to me, but I was certainly enjoying the sensation and I could barely wait to hear what Millie had arranged.

With the smile still intact, I made my way into the kitchen for breakfast.

Uneasy...

As it turned out, I did not see Millie at all for the next two weeks and for that matter, I barely heard from her either. Apparently, her grandmother was unwell and she had gone with her mom to help care for her. Then, just when I thought she was heading home again she was invited to stay with her cousins for a week. Hugely disappointed, I tried to keep busy and focus on the fun we would have together when she finally arrived back.

But I found it hard to be patient. I was so looking forward to meeting her friends and as well as that, I'd already become used to spending most days with her. Not having her around made me feel lonelier than ever and it was not a nice feeling at all.

I was also disappointed by her lack of texts. Although I'd sent several messages, I'd only received a few replies in return. Deep down, I knew that she was busy and probably didn't have time to be on her phone texting me. But it made me feel that I was much lower on her priority list than she was on mine. As much as I tried not to think that way, I couldn't help it.

However, after a couple of days of moping around the house, I received another message from Millie, explaining that she'd be back at the end of the week. Realizing that I'd been overreacting, I decided to find some things to do until she returned.

In a much better frame of mind, I decided to join my mom on a trip to the city. It was one place we had not yet visited and the day became even better when she suggested we check out the huge range of clothing shops on offer. That, of course, was the best part and the two of us ended up coming home with several new outfits. In particular, I especially loved the new black jeans that I'd found at one of the designer jeans stores but even after a whole day of shopping, I still hadn't found a top to match; there was a certain style that I was looking for but hadn't been able to find anything close.

One afternoon a few days later, I decided to wander down to the local mall to see if anything caught my eye. As it turned out, that day the area was extremely busy. Being summer holidays, there were lots of people about; parents with children, kids around my age, and teenagers hanging out and looking for something to do. I also discovered some free entertainment. As well as a couple of buskers, singing and playing instruments in the middle of the mall, there was a really cool street performer who was set up in a small amphitheater. He was performing on a circular stage area while all the spectators sat on the tiered steps that led down towards it.

His act had attracted a large audience and their cheering caught my attention. Deciding to stay and watch, I searched for a place to sit and then looked on while he set alight a number of juggling sticks and tossed them into the air, the flames soaring high into the sky. He then repeated his show by juggling a variety of odd shapes, all of this was done while riding around on a huge unicycle. This was a clever thing to do on its own, without having to juggle at the same time.

As well as his tricks, he was also a very funny comedian and the crowd was soon in fits of laughter. But when he moved onto his magic act and scanned the audience in search of a volunteer, I certainly did not expect to be the one chosen.

When I realized he was pointing at me, I stared towards the

ground and then at the people around me, hoping I was mistaken. When I didn't respond, I prayed that he'd overlook me and move onto someone else. I was not so lucky and when he called out loudly for the girl in the striped red and white T-shirt to come down and join him, I had no choice but to do as he'd asked.

I had no idea why he'd chosen me, especially as there was a stack of kids with their hands raised, desperate to be picked. Then I realized that it was all part of the act. He'd managed to gain the audience's attention and have everyone laughing at what he considered to be a funny joke, but it made me feel more awkward than ever. With their loud cheers encouraging me to take part, I was forced to make my way down the steps to the stage area below, all the while my face turning as red as the stripes on my T-shirt.

Making the situation even worse was a group of teenage boys who continued to cheer and whistle. Along with their yelling and cheering, they were making rude remarks. With every pair of eyes directed towards me, I was forced to stand by the performer's side. I desperately wished I could return to my seat.

All I could do though was look anxiously on as the performer shuffled a deck of very large, oversized playing cards and placed them in 3 separate piles on a table in front of us. He then demonstrated his trick by securing a thick, black blindfold around my head and selecting a random card that he then showed to the audience. Although I could not see a thing through the blindfold, I knew exactly what was going on in the performer's mind. The calling and cheering from the group of boys had continued and in my embarrassed state, I was alert to everything going on around me.

My mom and I often played card games together and I was

familiar with all the card names. Completely flustered and without thinking about what I was doing, I abruptly blurted out the name of the card in his hand.

"It's a red Queen of Diamonds."

"She guessed the card," called a man sitting nearby. "She must be able to see through the blindfold."

The performer looked towards me with a frown, obviously thinking that I'd peeked. He was then forced to check the blindfold was secured properly and demonstrate the trick again.

More embarrassed than ever, and finding it hard to believe that I had just announced the correct card name to the entire crowd, I purposely called out the wrong details next. The performer then repeated the trick himself, and after covering his own eyes with the blindfold was able to name the exact card that I'd chosen. This, of course, was all part of his magic act but I knew he was relieved when it was finally over and he was able to ask me to leave the stage.

With a confused and curious expression, he thanked me for participating. Still feeling embarrassed, I could not help but murmur a rude reply, "It's your fault! You shouldn't have chosen me in the first place!"

Ignoring the frown that appeared on his face, I made my way quickly back up to street level, at the same time, the cheers and whistles from the group of boys ringing loudly in my ears.

Keen to get as far away as possible, I headed through the crowded mall towards some fashion stores that I knew were situated at the other end. Standing outside one of the shops, I scanned the window display, wanting to catch my breath and try to forget about what had just happened. I had certainly not expected to become part of an embarrassing magic act when I'd left my house a couple of hours earlier.

Thankfully though, I noticed a pink midriff top hanging in a corner. Finally able to put the incident behind me, I focused on the pretty top instead. Staring at it some more, I tried to decide how it would look with my new jeans but then, unexpectedly, something else in the window happened to catch my attention.

With the bright sunlight shining on the glass, all I could see was a dark shape and at first, I thought it might be one of the teenagers from the amphitheater. But then I realized that the shape towered over my own reflection and was way too tall to be a kid. I'm not sure why it stood out but for some reason, I felt drawn to it.

As well as my ability to read people's minds, I had what my mom called the sixth sense. It wasn't completely reliable but right then, the familiar prickly feeling at the base of my neck was telling me that I definitely had something to worry about.

Turning abruptly, I found myself face to face with the one person I had hoped never to see again and I felt an instant chill work its way down my spine. Even though it was a warm and sunny afternoon, the goose bumps that appeared on my arms were causing me to shiver.

Wearing the same dark overcoat with the collar once again standing upright around his neck, the familiar but creepy figure did not budge from his spot. Instead, he stood staring back at me; the dark intense eyes, causing the hand of fear to claw at the pit of my stomach.

Where had he come from and what did he want? They were the questions racing through my head. But I did not dare to stop and focus on his thoughts. All I wanted was to get away as quickly as possible.

Breaking into a run, I headed out of the mall and down the street and I did not glance back until I was quite a distance away. A quick look behind assured me that he was no longer in sight and apart from a few people heading in the direction of the mall and some passing cars, there was no one else around.

Regardless, my heart continued to pound in my chest and I could feel its strong rhythm all the way to my front gate, where I was finally able to take a deep breath of relief.

When I raced up the front steps of the house, the door swung wide open and I stared in surprise at my mom, who was just about to head out the door.

"Where are you going?" I panted anxiously.

"I have to pick up some groceries for dinner," she replied with a frown. "Em, are you alright? You look like you've seen a ghost!"

"I'm okay. But I think I'll come with you!"

As grocery shopping was one thing I did not enjoy, she was certainly not expecting to hear those words from me. "Are you sure about that? Are you not feeling well, Emily?"

My mother only called me Emily if I was in trouble or there was a problem. And clearly she was expecting some type of explanation to help her understand why I'd suddenly be interested in grocery shopping, the thing I complained about most and usually tried to avoid.

"I'm just tired of being at home on my own," I lied, shooting her a quick grin as I headed back down the steps.

Reaching to open the door of the car, I jumped quickly

inside, hoping to avoid any more questions. The last thing I wanted was to worry her when there was more than likely a reasonable explanation.

Thinking some more about what had just happened, I considered all the details. The mall and shopping area were a perfect target for a thief, and that strange man probably hung out there regularly. There was sure to be an endless supply of distracted shoppers to steal from and I convinced myself that the chance meeting had been pure coincidence.

Perhaps he remembered me from the café and wanted revenge by giving me a scare. Well, he'd certainly done that and I hoped never to cross paths with him again.

As much as I wanted to believe that story though, I could not shake the feeling that there had to be something more.

Why had he stopped to stare at my reflection in the window?

And the evil glare he gave me when I turned to face him had made my skin crawl. He seemed to be looking into my soul, searching inside for answers. But answers to what?

I tried to push my next thought away but it was not easy. Especially because my intuition was telling me that the mysterious man in the shopping mall might be a mind reader as well.

Could it be at all possible?

Were there other people like me, people with the same powers and the same abilities?

And if that were the case, then why did he behave that way? It just did not make sense.

Sighing in frustration, I thought of my dad.

"What's going on, Dad? Please help me figure this out," I whispered the words silently in my head.

But for once this did nothing to ease my mind.

As hard as I tried, I was unable to ignore the familiar prickle that had once again appeared at the base of my neck.

The uncomfortable chill was working its way through my body and making me more uneasy than ever.

Excitement...

That evening, I helped Mom to prepare dinner. This was something I often did but on that night, in particular, it was a good distraction. Mom was trying out a new recipe and already the aroma coming from the pot on the stove was making my mouth water.

Completely focused on my job of peeling and chopping potatoes, the pinging sound of a text on my phone caught me by surprise. When I glanced at the screen and saw that it had come from Millie, I grabbed the phone in the desperate hope she had arrived back home.

"Good news? Mom asked as she eyed me curiously.

I looked towards her, the grin spreading wide on my face as I squealed loudly with delight. Millie had returned that afternoon and was inviting me to the movies the following day. That in itself was awesome news but what made it really special was the fact that Millie had been in contact with Jack and Blake and they were keen to go as well. It seemed that my wish was coming true and I could feel the joy inside me bubbling to the surface.

However, when I shared the news with Mom, I certainly did not expect the frown that appeared abruptly on her face.

"Who are Jack and Blake?"

Just as I opened my mouth to explain, she quickly interrupted.

"I'm glad to hear that you're making friends, Emmie, but I'm not happy about you heading off to the movies with a couple of boys I've never heard of. You haven't even mentioned them before. How do you know them and where are they from?"

"They're good friends of Millie's?" I stammered anxiously, gulping at the possibility of not being allowed to go.

"She's been friends with them for ages and she said they're really nice."

My mother's frown deepened as she looked at me suspiciously and I could see her brain ticking over. Anxious to know what was going on in her mind, I broke into her thoughts and alarm bells instantly started to ring in my own head.

She was wondering what I'd been up to that day and did not believe that I'd been hanging out at the mall on my own after all. I could feel my stomach drop as I realized she was planning to make me stay at home.

"Mom, come on!" I cried in exasperation. "I went to the mall to watch the street performers today and then I did some window shopping. That's all! Surely you're not going to say no!"

There was no way I wanted to mention anything else that had happened but I had to convince her to let me go to the movies. She had to let me go! She just had to!

"Jack and Blake are the boys from Millie's band," I continued, desperate to persuade her. "I already told you about the band she formed with her friend, Julia. You're always going on about me making some new friends. Now here's my chance. I can't believe you'd say no."

"And besides," I added quickly. "I'm twelve years old now. I'm not five anymore and you know I can look after myself!"

Her expression began to soften but she was still unsure.

"Em, I want you to stay safe. It's just the two of us and if anything happened to you, I don't know what I'd do."

I worry about you!

With a sigh, I moved towards her and gave her a firm hug. "Mom, nothing is going to happen to me. Moving here has been the best thing we've ever done. You said so yourself. I'm just going to the movies. It's no big deal. And I'll come straight home afterward if that's what you want."

I could see she was on the verge of agreeing but I could not risk the chance that she would still say no.

"If it makes you feel any better, you can drop me off and pick me up."

My pleading tone and final suggestion were the clinchers and I breathed a deep sigh of relief when she finally nodded her head.

"Alright, Emmie. I guess I have to let you grow up sometime. It's just happening too quickly!"

With the smile returning to my face I gave her another big hug of thanks then moved happily back to my spot at the kitchen bench. I tried to refocus on the potatoes I was chopping but could think of nothing else except the image of the two boys in Millie's photo. I could barely wait to meet them and I was sure they'd be every bit as nice as Millie had promised.

As well, I could not hide the fact that I found Jack very cute. I knew that Millie thought Blake was better looking but in my opinion, Jack was the one who stood out. There was something about his cheeky grin that I kind of adored and I was especially looking forward to meeting him.

Then, out of the blue, I realized I would have to decide on something to wear. Instantly, of course, the pink midriff top that I'd spotted that afternoon came to mind and I wished that I'd had the chance to buy it. Out of all my new clothes, my jeans and that top would probably be the prettiest outfit of all. But at least I did have other new things to choose from.

When dinner was over and I'd helped with the dishes, I was able to go to my room and decide. After trying on a couple of different combinations I decided on a white flared skirt and a pink top that had a pretty sequined love heart pattern on the front.

I noticed as I stared at my reflection in the mirror that the skirt kind of camouflaged how thin my legs were. Perhaps that style was best for me; either that or my mom's huge meals were finally having an effect.

Whatever the reason, I was able to climb into bed feeling happier than ever. The following day could not come quickly enough and the image that came to mind was similar to the one in Millie's photo frame. Except for one important detail.

Julia's face was replaced by my own.

Unexpected...

When I arrived at the cinema the next afternoon and found Millie waiting impatiently near the entrance, I could barely control my excitement.

Giving her a quick hug, I exclaimed with delight. "It's so good to see you!"

"You too, Em!" she grinned in return. "I'm so happy you could make it today! But I've got some bad news. The boys can't come!"

At the sound of her words, my smile instantly disappeared.

"Blake's grandparents turned up at his house this morning so he had to stay at home. And Jack didn't want to come without him."

I could feel my face fall; hugely disappointed, I could not believe what she had just told me.

"Oh, no!" I cried in dismay. "I was really looking forward to meeting them."

"Yeah, I know!" Millie replied. "I was looking forward to you meeting them as well. It's not fair Blake's grandparents decided to show up today! I was going to suggest we try for another day, but I it sounds like he has a lot of family stuff on right now. So I guess we'll just have to wait."

Trying hard to hide my disappointment, I reminded myself that at least I was still able to spend time with Millie, and I knew I should feel grateful for that.

In an effort to cheer me up, she continued, "Don't worry. We'll see them another time. We have the whole summer, remember?"

Giving my arm a quick squeeze, she smiled, "And besides, it gives me a chance to hang out with you. I've just had the most boring two weeks of my life and I'm so glad to be back!"

Following Millie to the ticket booth, I looked towards her curiously. From the texts she'd sent me, I had the impression she was having a great time while she was away, but I guessed I was wrong.

"You didn't have fun with your cousins?" I asked, a look of surprise on my face.

"Well, usually we have a great time together, but since they've moved to their country property, they've suddenly become obsessed with horses. I don't know where that came from because they've never even mentioned horses to me before. Now, horses are all they think about."

"Oh, wow!" I was more surprised at Millie's reaction than I was at anything else. To me, horses were amazing animals and I'd always dreamed of owning one. But it was clear that Millie wasn't interested in them at all.

"There's a fourteen-year-old girl who lives on the property next door and she has a couple of horses. Anyway, all they want to do is spend all day, every day at her place and now they're planning to get horses of their own. They don't talk about any else!" She rolled her eyes in disgust, clearly not happy about the situation.

"You obviously don't like horses, Millie!" I laughed in response.

This was one thing we did not have in common but her expressions were so funny, I couldn't help laughing.

"I'm kind of scared of them," she admitted abruptly, a serious frown appearing on her face.

In my mind, horses were the most beautiful creatures on the planet, so I found it hard to comprehend what she was saying.

"When I was nine, I went on a trail ride," she explained slowly. "It was my friend's birthday and there was a group of us. Everyone was really excited; all except me that was. I was feeling pretty nervous and I guess the horse I was riding picked up on that."

I followed Millie's words carefully, all the while, picturing the scene in my head.

"Anyway, my horse started trotting and I got scared and began to scream. The instructor told me later that my screaming must have spooked him because he took off through the bush. And all I could do was try to hang on!"

"Oh my gosh, that would have been terrifying!" I replied, "It's a wonder you didn't fall off! And you could've been really badly hurt!"

"I know," she replied with a sigh. "But I've never been on a horse since that day. And I don't think I'll be going back to my cousins' house in a hurry, either!"

I looked at her sympathetically, finally able to understand how she must feel. Although deep down, I still hoped that one day I might have a horse of my own.

At that point, however, we had finally reached the front of the queue and were able to buy our movie tickets. With that distraction, I thought our talk of horses would be over. But as we headed towards the cinema entrance, Millie had some more unexpected news to share.

"The worst part is that Julia is now getting a pony as well. I can't believe it! For the last two weeks, that's all she's talked about. Every time she rings me, it's horses, horses, horses. I was looking forward to visiting her but now I'm not so sure. Seriously, why am I surrounded by people who are obsessed with horses all of a sudden?

Then, eyeing me curiously, she continued, "Please don't tell me you plan to move to the country and get a horse too!"

Laughing in reply, I shook my head.

"To be honest, I'd love to have my own horse. But I can guarantee that's not going to happen; especially not anytime soon!"

"Thank goodness for that," she grinned.

I followed her thoughtfully through the door and into the darkness of the cinema beyond. Her sudden comment about Julia was surprising because she was previously so excited at the idea of visiting her; so much so that I'd become tired of hearing Julia's name constantly being mentioned.

It also seemed strange that I'd been wishing for Millie to stop dwelling on Julia, and instead, start focusing on her new friendship with me. Then all of a sudden, it seemed my wish might have come true.

Funnily enough, at that moment, I had no idea of another wish I'd been hoping for that was soon to become a reality as well.

And after my earlier disappointment, it came about much, much sooner than I had anticipated!

Feelings…

After the movie ended, Millie suggested we go for a wander through the mall and grab something to eat. Thankfully my mom had replied to my earlier text and agreed for me to stay out longer, which was great because I wanted to show Millie the midriff top I'd been eyeing off the day before.

While I still felt anxious about bumping into the creep who had scared me so much, I was determined that he would not stop me from having fun. As well, because I was with Millie I felt much safer than if I were on my own.

As it turned out Millie absolutely loved the top when I showed it to her in the store window. Then, when I tried it on along with a pair of jeans similar to the new ones I had recently bought, she insisted immediately that I should get it.

"Millie, that top looks stunning on you! And are those jeans the same as the ones you said you bought in the city?

When I nodded in reply, she exclaimed, "They're gorgeous! I'd like a pair like that myself."

Coming from Millie, this was a huge compliment. She had the most beautiful clothes and every time I saw her, she was wearing something really pretty. For her to compliment me on my choice of clothes was such a good feeling.

She'd already commented earlier on the outfit I was wearing that day as well, and instantly, her words had put a huge smile on my face.

"Ooh, I love your outfit, Emmie! Where did you get your

skirt? It looks so good on you!"

But it was the comment she made as I headed towards the shop counter with the midriff top in my hand that was the most special of all.

"You have the best figure, Emmie. You're so lucky!"

"What?" I replied, the shock causing me to repeat my question. "Who, me?"

"Yes, of course, you!" she laughed with a shake of her head. "Who else would I be talking about?"

Speechless and lost for words, I was unsure how to respond. No one had ever said anything like that to me before; except my mom that was. But my mom's comments didn't really count.

Because of the way I felt about my body, I was finding it hard to believe that Millie really meant what she had said, and although I'd promised myself several times that I would respect her privacy, this was one occasion where I could not resist checking to be completely sure.

In the past, I'd met girls who would say things but not really mean them. And it hurt so much to have them smile to my face but at the same time think horrible, mean thoughts in their heads.

"Those types of people are what you call two-faced," my mom had explained to me later.

And I soon learned the meaning of that expression. Those girls had a face they showed on the outside that was the one that everyone saw. But at the same time, they had another one hidden away inside.

They said one thing but really meant another.

Thankfully though, Millie was different. It had only taken a second or two to read her mind and I had all the reassurance I needed. She seemed to say exactly what she was thinking. And it was her next thought that completely changed my life.

"I don't think Emmie has any idea of how pretty she is. And she's such a nice person! I'm so lucky to have her as my friend!"

When I heard those words silently spoken inside Millie's head, I did a double take and stared intently towards her. But she simply smiled back; that wonderful, genuine smile that I had come to know. And instantly my heart welled with happiness.

To Millie, I was not a gawky, skinny freak. I did, in fact, look good in the clothes I wore, and she was happy to have me as her friend.

Right then, I thought my day could not get any better.

But then as is sometimes the case, something completely unexpected happened.

And when I later thought about the chance meeting, I wondered if some things were just meant to be.

A crush...

Recalling his startled look of surprise as he stared at me then at Millie and back to me again, I was convinced that my heart had definitely skipped a beat.

Jack was the cutest looking boy I had ever come across. When I lay in bed that night and thought about the moment Millie and I had spotted him in the mall, I felt a small flutter in my stomach.

"Is that Jack?" I had asked Millie, as I tried not to stare in his direction.

He had been standing on the outskirts of a circle of families and kids being entertained by yet another street performer. This one, however, was a young rap singer, and the sound of his music had immediately caught our attention.

It had obviously caught Jack's as well and I watched him from a distance as he stood mesmerized by the teenager blasting out the words of the latest rap tune. It sounded so cool. The rhythm combined with the lyrics created a really catchy effect and the entire crowd was fascinated.

"OMG! It is Jack!" Millie responded with surprise. "That's amazing! How did you know it was him?"

Turning a slight shade of red, I did not want to admit that I'd been obsessing over his image from the day she had shown me the group photo; so much so that I had recognized him immediately.

The moment the rapper finished his song, Jack happened to turn our way, almost as though he could feel someone watching him. That was when I caught sight of the brown eyes that had stood out so dramatically in the photo. But feeling the blush on my skin deepen, I looked quickly away.

"Oh my gosh. He saw me staring. How embarrassing!"

The words raced through my head while at the same time, I tried to comprehend the fact that he was right there in our midst.

Then, when Millie called out to him and he headed over, I could feel my stomach doing somersaults as I stood nervously by her side.

When Millie introduced me, I tried not to be awkward but I was struggling to act normally. He was even better looking in real life and I could not take my eyes off his cheeky grin.

He seemed to be staring at me as well and I wondered for a moment what he was thinking. Was it good or bad? Right then, I had to know and could not resist the temptation to find out. With the butterflies fluttering wildly inside me, I concentrated on his thoughts and instantly felt my face turn even redder.

"She's so pretty! Maybe I should've gone to the movies after all!"

Looking quickly away, I focused on Millie. Then in the next breath, I began to build the invisible brick wall in my mind, the one that I knew for sure, needed to be built as quickly as possible.

If I were going to have any chance of acting normally around him, I had to block his thoughts. But I needed help. For some reason, where Jack was concerned, the temptation to read his mind was just too much for me to control. And as I focused on piling the bricks, one on top of the other, I avoided all eye contact with the boy at my side.

A few minutes later, when I'd finally begun to relax, Millie suggested that we grab a table and something to eat. With the cheeky grin remaining fixed to his face, Jack instantly agreed. So we quickly found a place to sit and ordered our food.

Millie had not seen Jack since Julia had left town and obviously had lots to catch up on. This gave me the chance to listen in while the two of them reminisced about their last days of school before the summer break. They had shared so many memories with Julia and Blake and I could not help but feel envious about the fun things they'd all been a part of.

One, in particular, was their band. The fact that they'd been asked to perform at their graduation ceremony, seemed the coolest thing ever. Watching the two friends as they chatted and laughed, I could see how special their years together at Carindale Middle School had been. Whereas my school life had passed by in a blur; too many schools, too many "fake" friends and too many sad memories.

If only my mom and I had moved to Carindale sooner, the previous years of my life could have been so different. But then I remembered about Julia, and I realized that the opportunity to become a part of this incredible group of friends would never have happened anyway.

As I lay on my bed later that evening thinking back over the afternoon, I thought again of Jack's smiling face and the constant laughter from all of us. He was one of the funniest people I'd ever met and apart from being extremely good-looking, he also seemed to be a really nice person.

But then another thought occurred to me, one that had crossed my mind earlier but had been brushed aside; probably because I didn't want to acknowledge it or believe that it might be true.

Millie had mentioned a previous crush. And although she said she didn't feel that way about Jack anymore, I wondered if that were really the case.

The two seemed to get on very well. Obviously, they'd been good friends for a long time, and it showed. They also had their singing in common and were now talking about catching up for a rehearsal to work on some of their old songs. There was an upcoming competition that Jack was planning to enter, and he was encouraging Millie to do the same.

According to Jack, Millie had an amazing voice and at the same time, Millie explained how awesome Jack was as a rapper. It was so great to see each of them encouraging the other. But was there really something more?

I'd never asked Millie about her friendship with Jack. She'd simply told me that Julia and Blake were going out and were still really close, even though she'd moved away. She had never given any other details and I hadn't asked.

I could feel my smile fading. The more I thought about the way Millie had acted around Jack, the more uneasy I felt.

There was a solution though. For me, it was quite simple.

My mom always said that I had powers for a reason.

And at least that way, I would know for sure what was really going on in my friend's head; and Jack's too for that matter.

When I pictured his cheeky grin as he said goodbye, I felt the small flutter in my stomach once again. I just hoped that I was wrong about Millie and that things could work out perfectly for me for a change.

Apart from a dorky looking kid who was nice to me back in fourth grade, I had never had a real crush on a boy.

At my last school, many of the girls in my class had boyfriends and all they'd talk about during their lunch breaks were boys.

In the end, I grew tired of it all and just tended to keep to myself. They preferred it that way though and were more than happy when I'd disappear to the library during lunch breaks.

But all of a sudden, I did have a boy to think about. And I was certain that even though we'd only just met, he quite liked me as well.

I then remembered that Millie's friendship was much more important to me than a silly crush. And when Jack's smiling face came to mind once again, I pushed the image out of my head.

All I could do was hope that things would work out in the end.

They just had to.

Millie's news...

When I saw Millie a couple of days later, it was at my house. I had originally hoped that we'd spend the afternoon together and then have a sleepover. But Millie had already planned to catch up with Jack for a rehearsal, so by the time she arrived it was late afternoon. As soon as I heard her knock, I raced to open the door and found her bouncing on the spot with excitement.

The competition was scheduled for the following month and both Millie and Jack had registered an entry in the solo division. It was the very first time for this event in Carindale and apparently, heaps of people of different ages were planning to take part. Millie blurted out all the details, her level of excitement rising with every word.

"Carindale's Got Talent" posters were popping up everywhere. And because of the overwhelming demand, they had decided to have two categories, one for younger kids and one for teenagers and adults.

As Millie and Jack were both thirteen, they were eligible for the 13 Years and under division, which was very lucky. Otherwise, they'd be competing against hugely talented people like the rapper we'd seen in the mall. Millie and Jack obviously had a much better chance against younger kids, although they would still be competing against each other.

But this didn't seem to bother either of them in the slightest. In fact, all they were concerned about was encouraging each other to do their best. It was all that Millie could talk about and her rehearsal with Jack that afternoon had made her more eager than ever.

When my mom overheard all the excited chatter coming from the living room, she sat down to join us, hugely interested in hearing about the competition Millie had entered. She was also interested in hearing Millie sing.

This had taken a little convincing, and at first, Millie refused, using the excuse, "I'm too shy!"

But I simply laughed off that remark because I knew for a fact, she was definitely not shy. Besides that, she had performed in front of large crowds before, including the whole of Carindale Middle School at her graduation. So, surely she could sing for my mom and me in the safety of our small living room!

While I was expecting that Millie would sound quite good, I was certainly not prepared for the voice that exploded from her lips when she began her song. She was singing along with the music that I had downloaded on iTunes and we could hear the words clearly through the speakers sitting in the corner of the room. However, it took only a few seconds for her to become more confident and then the music from the speakers was completely muffled by the power of her voice.

Sitting alongside my mom on the sofa, we both looked on in awe. My arms seemed to be covered in goose bumps and when I noticed the prickly feeling, I realized that the hairs on my arms were also standing on end.

The moment the song ended, the surprise on my mom's face was obvious in her voice as well. "Millie that was incredible!"

"Oh my gosh, Millie!" I squealed in shock. "You are amazing!!!"

Smiling broadly, she looked at each of us in turn. "Do you

really think so?"

I could see that her question was genuine. Even though she must surely have been told endless times before that she had a great voice, she was still disbelieving. Or perhaps she was just being modest, but when we nodded our heads and raved about how much we loved the tone of her voice, she beamed happily with thanks.

"Sing something else," I begged. "Please, Millie. You are so good!"

"Yes, Millie, choose another song. This is fabulous!" My mom was clearly enjoying Millie's performance as much as myself, and I smiled widely at her reaction.

Millie grinned at the two of us and needed no further encouragement to begin another song, explaining that she needed help deciding which one to choose for the competition.

So we listened carefully, but it quickly became obvious that it was not an easy decision to make. While Mom liked the first, I thought that the second one sounded better. As it was one of my favorite top ten songs though, I was probably biased and we could not come to an agreement. Then I reminded Millie that she still had four weeks to decide.

But my mom continued prattling on about Millie's voice and other suggestions for songs that she might like to consider. I could see that she was not helping the situation and besides that, I was desperate to grab Millie and head to my room, so that we could have some time to ourselves.

My mother loved talking, probably because she spent her days on the computer and didn't often get the chance to meet people in person. Whenever she started speaking, it was always hard to get a word in.

She also loved asking questions; the most random things would sometimes come from her mouth and I'd often roll my eyes with embarrassment. Whenever I complained about her habit, she'd remind me that it was the only way to get to know a person.

That afternoon was no different. From the moment Millie had walked in the front door Mom had barely stopped talking. So I knew I had to step in. At the first opportunity, I caught Millie's attention and we eventually managed to slip away. I was desperate to hear all about her afternoon at Jack's and could not get to my room quickly enough.

Jack's smiling face had been stuck in my head for the past two days and I wanted to reach into Millie's thoughts. That was my way of finding out about people, and I knew that it was often the only way to hear the truth. Asking questions, the way my mom tended to do, did not always work. Whereas my method was kind of foolproof.

As it turned out, I managed to find out a lot more information that I had previously anticipated.

Emotions...

It became immediately obvious that Jack had not only been on my mind but on Millie's as well. While this was to be expected, especially after they'd spent all afternoon rehearsing together, I could see that Millie's thoughts went even deeper.

Although I tried, I could not prevent the uncomfortable feeling of disappointment. But there was also something else. If I were to be completely honest, I'd be forced to admit there was another emotion I was feeling quite intensely right then. And it was one I'd become familiar with over the years.

On so many occasions in the past, I had stood back and watched other girls with their close knit groups; all such good friends, hanging out, doing fun stuff together, laughing, joking, sharing secrets, having fun. And there I was, the weird loner, or loser, I should probably say, on my own as usual.

Time and time again, I could not help the emotion that had forced its way to the surface. It wasn't nice and I wasn't proud of it. Regardless, however, I was unable to prevent it.

That emotion was a word beginning with the letter J.

A capital J.

And that's what I called it...the J word.

My mom told me once that Jealousy was a curse. And I found out for myself that she was right. Because jealousy made me miserable. And right at that moment, there it was again. Only this time, it wasn't because I did not have a best friend to hang out with. I'd found a best friend but quite unexpectedly, something else had caused that cursed feeling to rear its ugly head once more.

And oddly enough, on this occasion, the Jealousy curse was having the exact same effect as it had in the past; a dark, sickly feeling in the bottom of my stomach and in the back of my head. I could feel the throbbing of its pulse as I sat listening to the words coming from Millie's mouth.

"Jack sounded so good today! You should've heard him, Emmie. His voice is even better than before."

"He's been practicing heaps and it really shows. I've already told him he's going to win. But he doesn't believe me. He's convinced that I'll win!"

"I love singing and so does Jack. It's awesome!"

Millie laughed happily, the delight obvious on her face. She could not stop talking about him and it did not take a mind reader to work out what she was thinking.

"Jack, Jack, Jack..."

I knew I should be happy for her. I knew that he was her friend. I also knew that they'd been friends forever. Whereas I had only just met him.

It was almost comical really; that I should feel so intensely about someone I had only met once and happened to spend a couple of hours with. But for some reason, we seemed to click. And I felt more comfortable with him than I had felt with anyone ever before. Perhaps even more so than with Millie.

"You're pathetic Emily!" I spoke the words harshly in my head, reprimanding myself for being such a loser.

"You've just met the guy and look at you! What a joke!"

And then, when I thought that things could not get any worse, Millie proceeded to share some more startling news.

And the wretched feeling in the pit of my stomach suddenly became much worse.

Shock...

"Jack and I came up with the most incredible idea!" Millie was so excited about her news and I sat on my bed trying to focus on her words, all the while attempting to ignore the sick feeling that was taking over my whole body.

"Carindale's Got Talent has become so popular they've decided to add a new category to each age group." Millie continued on with her spiel and I continued on with my efforts to follow what she was saying.

"Instead of combining all the solo and group performances together, they now have two sections, one for solo artists and one for groups. Apparently, there are a few dance troupes entering with twelve or more dancers in each. As well there's a couple of bands and some other group acts. So it wouldn't be fair for people on their own to compete against them."

She paused briefly to take a breath.

"Anyway, Jack came up with the idea of getting together with Blake and entering the group section. Blake is an incredible drummer and we sound so amazing when we perform together. And then I thought of the biggest brain wave. At first, I didn't think it would be impossible, but then I decided it wouldn't hurt to ask."

Pausing for effect, she added with a huge grin, "So I made a phone call."

Right then, I really did not want to hear all the details. So much talk about the competition that she and Jack were entering together was making me feel more Jealous than ever.

Millie had already asked if I wanted to enter. "Is there something you're good at Emmie? Something that you could do, so you could enter as well?"

If only she knew!

"Yes, I actually do have a talent, Millie. And my talent is so spectacular that I'm sure I would win!"

I imagined myself responding to her question. And I also imagined her look of disbelief as she listened to my answer. The idea of a genuine mind reader was too much for anyone to believe in. A person who could focus on the thoughts of any person at all in the audience, and share exactly what they were thinking…a color, a number, the time they went

to bed the night before, what they had for breakfast. You name it, a proper mind reader could tell you all the details.

And I was that person.

But could I enter a competition with my talent?

Of course not!

Refocusing on Millie's moving lips right then, I realized abruptly that she'd just said something I really should have been listening to.

"I made a phone call," she had said.

Those were her words but what had she said afterward….

It was something about Julia. Something that was making me more uneasy than ever.

So I asked her to repeat it.

"Sorry, Millie. I didn't catch that. Who did you decide to ring?"

And I listened as Millie's voice rose with excitement. She

was so excited that she was on her feet, jumping up and down and almost bursting with joy.

I knew deep down that I should be excited too. I knew that I should feel happy for her.

But that prickly sensation at the base of my neck, the one I felt when I knew that something bad was going to happen, was making me feel otherwise.

And try as I might to join in her excitement, it was just not possible.

Changes...

The following evening, I received a call from Millie. And her news was exactly as I had expected.

"Emmie, Julia just called me back and guess what! She's allowed to come! Can you believe it? She asked her parents and at first, they said no. But then she begged and begged. She even told them she'd use her own savings to pay for the airfare. And it just so happens that there's a sale on flights right now. It's meant to be!"

Barely taking a breath, Millie continued, her voice becoming an excited jumble of words, "So now we'll be able to enter our band in Carindale's Got Talent. And you'll get to meet Julia, Emmie. You're going to love her; I know you will. This is the best news ever!"

She was practically screaming into the phone and I had to hold it away from my ear as she spoke.

"I almost didn't bother asking her, Em. She only left town a few weeks ago and I thought there'd be no way she'd be allowed to come back so soon. Plus, there's the pony thing that she's been so obsessed with. But she said she'll just put off getting a horse until she gets back. And because she's been missing us all so much and it's also the summer holidays, her parents finally gave in!!"

"That's so good, Millie." I tried to sound enthusiastic. I really did try, but I could not escape the sinking feeling that was taking hold.

Millie had talked about Julia so much and I was sure that she was every bit as nice as Millie said.

Julia...
she looked so nice in Millie's photos!

But what would she think of me?

And the one question I had not been brave enough to ask was, "How long is she staying for?"

If it were for the rest of the summer, then I was doomed. I just knew it.

To begin with, she was arriving in a few days and staying at Millie's house. She would be with her every single day and every single night. There'd be no time for me. And if I were Julia, I'm quite sure I wouldn't want to be sharing my best friend with some strange new girl who had recently moved into town and decided to take my place.

The photo of the four friends flashed into my thoughts.

Millie, Julia, Jack and Blake, standing side by side, best friends forever. And to think that I'd hoped to become a part of that group, and most importantly, to replace the girl who had left. What a pipe dream that was!

It was clearly not going to happen. Certainly not that summer anyway.

I'd been so excited about the weeks ahead. It was going to be the best summer I'd ever had. And then, almost overnight everything had changed.

Julia was due to arrive in a few days; not a few weeks, but a few days! Just my luck that the sale on airfares happened to be for that week only. The four friends would be reunited. And with the competition only a few weeks away they would spend their time rehearsing; as well as fitting in a heap of other fun stuff, I was sure.

And as for me?

Well, the picture I was painting in my head right then, was blank; an empty canvas. No color, no fun, no friends.

Just one lonely girl with a so-called miracle gift. One that was so miraculous it had to be kept intact, locked away in a secret place for safe keeping.

"You're so lucky to have that gift, Emmie." My mother's words rang in my head.

But right then, I would do anything to trade my gift for the one thing I truly wanted.

The one thing that had been within my grasp just the day before, to be whisked away once again.

Feeling thankful...

As I held the phone in my hand, something about Millie's tone made me refocus on what she was saying. I hadn't realized but she'd moved on from the excitement of Julia's arrival and was actually inviting me to hang out the next day.

I blinked a few times as a glimmer of hope registered in my mind.

Millie seemed aware of my thoughts and how I was feeling. Her reassuring words were reaching through the phone and although I was unable to read her mind right then, the message came through loud and clear.

She was not going to suddenly ditch me the moment Julia arrived. But instead, was already planning for us to meet and for the three of us to do some fun things together.

"I've told Julia all about you, Emmie, and she's really looking forward to meeting you! I'm sure you'll get on really well."

I listened carefully as she chatted on, my hopes beginning to soar. Maybe things would be okay after all. Perhaps I was spending too much time expecting the worst when it didn't need to be that way.

After all, up until the day before, I'd felt certain that Millie was a genuine friend. My gut instinct had told me so. For once in my life, I just needed to believe in myself. And I also needed to believe in Millie.

Then, as if to prove a point about her friendship being real, she was asking what I was up to the following day.

And a short while later, with an unexpected grin on my face, I found myself searching my cupboard for something suitable to wear.

Her invitation had come as a complete surprise. Totally unexpectedly, she had suggested we spend the day at one of the local theme parks. There were a couple of major ones nearby, I had seen them advertised on television. I'd certainly hoped to have the opportunity to go one day, but had definitely not expected it would be so soon.

And the idea that Millie was going to extra lengths to do something really fun with me before Julia arrived, was all I needed to put the smile back on my face. That meant more to me than anything.

That and the fact that she had two double passes which she could have saved for Julia's arrival; the two girls could easily have gone with Jack and Blake and I was certain that Julia would have loved that. But instead, Millie had decided otherwise.

She invited me for a sleepover at her house afterward and I quickly agreed.

After ending the call, I took a deep breath and glanced towards the photo of my dad that sat alongside my bed.

"Thanks, Dad!" I whispered quietly.

And as I looked lovingly into the eyes of the handsome man staring back, I knew that he was there.

He was with me every step of the way, I just needed to remember that, and everything would be okay.

Smiling gratefully at him once more, I turned back towards the cupboard to continue my search for the clothes I would need for the following couple of days.

Millie and her mom would be arriving early to pick me up and I wanted to be sure that I was ready.

An unexpected guest...

I had not been to a theme park since the time my mom took me for my sixth birthday. But at that stage, I was too young to go on all the big scary rides. I remember staring in awe as the roller coaster zoomed past us at break neck speed, the kids screaming and yelling as they clung tightly to the handrails.

To me, it was the most thrilling ride I could ever imagine and I dreamed of being able to ride it myself when I was old enough.

That day, my childhood dream came true. The roller coaster proved to be every bit as thrilling as I had imagined and just as I'd pictured in my head, I found myself clinging to the handrails in the exact same manner as the kids I'd watched when I was seven. And my screams were every bit as loud.

It was everything I'd hoped and when the ride ended, Millie and I raced towards the end of the queue so we could have another turn.

By the end of the day, we'd been on almost every scary ride we could find. It was the most fun I had ever had and when we hopped into Millie's mom's car later that afternoon, we were both bursting with stories about our fantastic day.

Just as we neared Millie's house, the sudden pinging noise from a text on her phone sounded loudly in the car. From my place alongside her on the backseat, I saw Jack's name appear in clear view on the screen. Quickly reading his message, she looked towards me with a grin.

"How would you feel about Jack coming over tonight? The other day he was complaining about being bored and I said he should come to my house for a movie and pizza sometime. But if you'd rather he didn't then that's fine, I'll just tell him to come another night."

"I don't mind at all," I replied smiling towards her.

"I didn't think you would," her grin widened as she asked her mom for permission to have one extra for dinner.

"That's fine, girls," Mrs. Spencer replied, in her usual cheery manner. "We'll just have to order extra pizza."

Looking towards Millie, I wondered curiously about what she'd just said. I really wasn't sure what she meant by that. But I had already promised myself to stay out of her head. I had the invisible brick wall in place and I was determined that it should stay there. Millie was being such a good friend and she deserved that respect.

But then she made another comment about how much fun it was going to be when Jack arrived, and I really didn't need to read her mind to work out what she was thinking.

The dreamy look on her face as she smiled happily, said it all.

Truth...

As promised, Jack brought over a selection of movies. But all of them were action types and sci-fi, something we weren't expecting.

"Typical boy movies," Millie laughed as she looked through the pile.

We had cartons of pizza sitting on the glass-topped coffee table in front of us and were set up ready to go. All we needed to do was agree on a movie. In the end, we chose a latest release science fiction horror type, one that I was particularly interested in seeing because my mom had never let me watch anything other than PG movies before.

For me, this was going to be a first; not only the M rated movie but also the fact that I was having a sleep-over at a friend's house and a really cute boy was joining us for a few hours.

I'd already accepted the idea that Jack was Millie's friend and if she had a crush on him then I would just have to deal with it. There was no way I wanted to risk our friendship and besides, the two of them had so much in common, I guessed that they were destined to be together.

I kept my own crush hidden just below the surface, determined to keep it a secret. This was something I had experience with. I'd been keeping secrets my whole life, and this occasion was no different.

Thankfully, I'd also managed to hide away the cursed Jealous streak that I'd been attacked with a few days earlier. And rather than letting it fill me with pain and misery, I'd pushed it away right out of reach.

I could not help the fact that I liked Jack. He was so good looking and so much fun to be around. But Millie obviously thought so too. I just had to remind myself that her friendship mattered much more than a sudden boy crush.

One thing I had noticed though was his huge grin the moment he arrived and from that minute onwards, there had seemed to be a kind of connection between us. We really did get on extremely well; it was almost as though I'd known him forever.

Something told me that he felt it too. It was like an easy comfortable feeling that just seemed right. And if I had to keep my crush secret, at least I could try to enjoy simply hanging out with him as a friend.

Trying not to focus on the crush issue, I sat down alongside Millie, leaving room on the other side of her for Jack. She'd been drooling over him since he arrived and I did not want to get in the way. After dimming the lights a little, we settled down to watch the movie, all the while munching on the delicious pizza in front of us.

Throughout the film, Jack continued to startle both Millie and me; calling out and making loud noises right at the scariest moments, causing us to jump from our seats in fright. Laughing hysterically to himself, he sat prepared for each scary scene. As he had already seen the movie before, he knew exactly what was coming up next.

I was grateful for his humor though as it eased the tension in the room as well as the fact that I'd been clinging to my seat most of the time, unwilling to admit how scared I was.

Then, as soon as the movie ended, Millie stood up from her spot on the couch, brightened the lights and suggested we play a game instead.

"That's a great idea," I replied, smiling in agreement. I'd seen enough scary movies for one night and was more than happy to do something else. "What game do you have in mind?"

I was certainly not prepared for her response though and felt a small quiver of anxiety when she announced her choice.

"Truth or Dare!" she exclaimed excitedly, looking from Jack to me and back to him again.

"Sure!" Jack responded, "That sounds like fun!"

Hesitantly, I joined them on the floor as they sat cross-legged in the middle of the room. Although I'd heard of the game, I'd never played it myself, but for some reason, I felt slightly uneasy about what lay ahead.

The first few questions were quite harmless and within minutes we were all rolling around on the carpet in fits of laughter.

"Jack, I dare you to put on my mom's gardening hat then go downstairs and tell her how much you love it."

"What?" he replied, shaking his head in denial, as he stared in horror at the object sitting in view on top of a nearby cupboard. "She'll think I'm a freak! There's no way I can do that and keep a straight face."

"You have to!" she laughed. "It's my turn to give you a dare. And you have to do it!"

I joined in the laughter as we watched him put the large pink hat topped with fake flowers and other strange bits and pieces onto his head and make his way down the stairs.

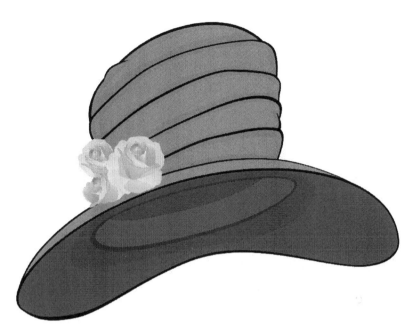

It was one of the funniest things I'd ever seen and when he came back, his face bright red with embarrassment, I demanded that he put the hat back on so I could take a photo.

The game continued, with each of us giving each other crazy dares that made us all clutch our stomachs, the wild laughter creating sharp pangs of pain that we could not avoid.

But then the game turned more serious with Millie's next question. "Em, Truth...how old were you when you had your first kiss from a boy?"

Blushing deeply, I glanced back at her with a small shake of my head. "I've never been kissed by a boy."

I could feel Jack staring my way, but I did not return his gaze. The question was embarrassing but I think I was more embarrassed about having to admit that I'd never been kissed. Instead, I looked down at the carpet, and fumbled through my brain, trying to think of a Truth question to ask him that wasn't quite so personal. Anything to change the subject and remove the attention from me.

"Jack, Truth…do you think Millie has a good voice?"

I grinned his way, knowing already what his answer would be. It was an easy question and he looked gratefully back as he answered. "I think Millie has an awesome voice!"

Alright, it's my turn again, Millie interrupted, as she turned quickly towards me, "Em, Truth…name the boy you have a crush on right now?"

Immediately feeling my face turns an even darker shade of red, I glanced quickly at Jack before looking at Millie once more.

How was I going to answer that? We'd all agreed to follow the rules and that meant being completely honest with our answers. But there was no way I could tell the truth. Why did Millie decide to ask me that?

But deep down inside I knew. She was aware of my feelings and once again, I felt convinced that she was able to reach into my thoughts as easily as I could reach into hers. Perhaps it was simply because we'd become close friends and she'd come to recognize what was going on in my head. Or was my face an open book? A place that showed all my inner most feelings, the ones that I desperately tried to keep secret.

Whatever it was, it was unnerving just the same.

And it gave me a very clear idea of how kids had felt in the past when they realized that I knew exactly what they were thinking.

Yes, it was creepy.

Yes, it was uncomfortable.

And, no, I did not like it. Not one little bit.

My head spun as I searched wildly for an answer.

But then, as if saved by some unseen miracle, Mrs. Spencer abruptly appeared at the top of the stairs. "Jack, your dad just pulled up in his car. It's quite late. You'd better not keep him waiting."

And gulping in relief, I watched as Jack jumped quickly to his feet; the expression of relief evident on his face as well.

After one last glance in my direction, he looked towards Millie and then her mom, thanking them both for having him and then gathered up his movies and made his way down the stairs.

Following him to the doorway, we waved goodbye as we watched the car pull away.

"He's such a nice young boy!" Mrs. Spencer exclaimed from her spot behind us.

"Yes, he is," Millie replied, as we closed the door and made our way back up the stairs.

She did not mention her Truth question again, and for that I was grateful.

But I was convinced she already knew the real answer.

The arrival...

The next few days flew quickly by and before I knew it, Saturday morning had arrived and I was sitting at home on my own, trying to find something to keep busy, anything at all to occupy myself and to stay distracted.

At the exact same time I was well aware that Millie, Jack, and Blake were all in Mrs. Spencer's car, headed towards the airport. Julia's plane would arrive in exactly one hour and they had left early in order to find a car park and to be there waiting when she walked through the arrival gates.

Millie had already told me the details of their surprise welcome. Julia was only expecting Millie to be at the airport with her mom and had no idea that the boys would be there as well.

I could easily picture the scene as the three friends rushed towards Julia, throwing their arms around her in a huge welcoming hug. And I could also imagine the reunion between her and Blake, who according to Millie, was the love of Julia's life.

Sighing to myself, I moped around the house...the memory of Millie's promise ringing in my ears.

"Emmie, you'll have to come over to my house so you can meet Julia. I'll find out what's happening with rehearsals and then I'll text you. Hopefully, we can arrange a time for Monday. Unless you have something else planned?"

"No, that sounds great, Millie," I had replied, knowing full well that I would not be busy. I had no plans whatsoever.

My mom didn't usually work on weekends but that morning she had a ton of paperwork to catch up on, so I waited impatiently for her to finish so we could head out together and do something. Anything to take my mind off what I could not stop thinking about.

With nothing else to do, I spent the morning looking at YouTube videos and checking out online shopping websites. These were something that Millie had introduced me to and although I'd already spent the clothing allowance my mom had given me, it was fun to look anyway. And besides that, it helped to pass the time.

After a while, I decided to check my Instagram feed, knowing full well that Millie would be sure to post a photo of Julia once she'd arrived. And sure enough, it popped up instantly; a picture of a really pretty girl with long brown hair and beautiful big eyes. She was wearing a gorgeous green skirt and a black and white crop top. Millie stood alongside her and the pair had their arms wrapped around each other in a welcoming hug. It was such a great pic and clearly showed how happy they were to be together again.

But it was the post underneath that tore at my heart the most…

Amazing to be with my best friend again! Welcome back, Julia! I've missed you so much!

@juliajones

With another deep sigh, I tossed my phone down onto the bed and reached for my teddy. Right then, I just needed a hug. He was always there for me and hugging him always helped.

But that morning as I clutched him tightly to my chest, I could feel the tears drip slowly down my cheeks. I knew I was being silly. I knew I was being childish and I knew I was being selfish. They had every right to enjoy their time together. And I had no right to complain.

But right then I didn't care.

Completely still, I sat quietly in that very spot and remained there without moving until I heard my mom's voice calling me into the kitchen for lunch.

Dread...

Finally, Monday arrived and as promised, Millie's text appeared on my phone but it was not what I'd been hoping for.

So sorry Emmie, can we hang out another day this week? Julia and I are so busy with stuff that we won't have any spare time today. But she is dying to meet you! Talk soon! Xxx

Hugely disappointed, I did not want to stay in the house with nothing to do. So I asked for permission to head into the mall and made plans to meet my mom later for lunch.

I'd browsed the shops in that mall so many times, that I knew them back to front. Luckily though, the paved area was bustling with a variety of street entertainers, some of whom I'd seen before but also a couple of new ones.

The sweet sound of a girl singing and playing guitar caught my attention and I headed in the direction of her voice. I could see that a huge crowd had gathered and I wondered absently if she was also planning to enter Carindale's Got Talent.

As I moved closer and found a spot amongst the crowd where I was able to get a better view, I realized with a surprised gasp that Millie and Jack were standing amongst the audience on the opposite side of the circle. And when I took a closer look, I caught sight of a really pretty girl alongside them.

When I watched Millie turn towards her with a smile,

obviously commenting on the singer, I saw the girl next to her smile in return, her beautiful features lighting her face.

So that was Julia. I could clearly see in that instant, that she was even prettier than in her photographs.

A boy who I assumed was Blake stood behind her; all four were captivated by the singing of the girl, whose amazing voice was attracting loud applause from the entire crowd.

While I pretended to watch the girl's performance, my focus was on the group of friends on the other side. I could not take my eyes from them.

As I stood there, I began to sense the familiar prickle of discomfort on the back of my neck and I froze in my place; the sight of Millie, Jack and the others standing amongst the crowd on the other side, momentarily forgotten.

Not daring to turn around, I kept my focus ahead, feeling sure that the mysterious, creep of a man had found me yet again. But then, unable to stand still and do nothing, I slowly scanned the area behind me, expecting to see his glaring eyes on mine at any moment. Surprisingly, however, he was nowhere to be seen.

The prickling sensation continued, and feeling alert and afraid, I looked around once more. That was when I noticed a boy around my age standing nearby. What caught my attention was his intense gaze as he stared directly across the circle. However, his eyes were not on the singer, but instead, he looked directly towards the crowd on the other side.

He had no idea that I'd noticed him but I could feel the hatred dripping from his evil scowl. Pushing through to the thoughts in his head, I gasped with shock, the words I was hearing filling me with dread.

"Julia Jones! What are you doing back in town? And you're still hanging out with that loser! Do you seriously think I'm going to let you get away with what you did? I haven't forgotten. And your time will come."

My mouth agape, I stood motionless and in shock. What was going on? Why did he hate Julia so much? And who was the person he was referring to? He was calling one of them a loser and I had no idea who. What I was completely sure of though was that he'd meant every word he had said.

Then, as he turned abruptly around and moved away from the crowd, I watched him disappear down the length of the mall; all the while his intense hatred lingering in the air.

With a sickly feeling, I looked again towards the group opposite.

And taking a deep breath, I tried to calm my racing pulse.

***

Find out what happens next in

Mind Reader

Book 2

AVAILABLE NOW!

You can also read

MIND READER: Part One – Books 1, 2 & 3

at a *DISCOUNTED PRICE!*

Follow me on Instagram @juliajonesdiary

And please LIKE Julia Jones' Facebook page to be kept up to date with all the latest books in the Julia Jones and Mind Reader series…

https://www.facebook.com/JuliaJonesDiary

Thank you for reading my book.

If you liked it, could you please leave a review?

Thanks so much!

Katrina x

Have you read the Julia Jones' Diary series yet?

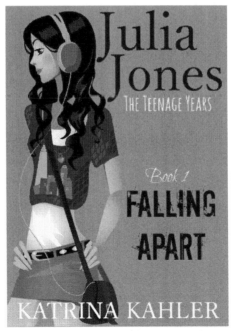

You can also buy these books as a collection at a
DISCOUNTED PRICE!

Many of the following books can also be purchased as a combined set so that you can read the entire collection at a DISCOUNTED PRICE!
Just search for the titles on Amazon or your favorite online book retailer to see what is available...

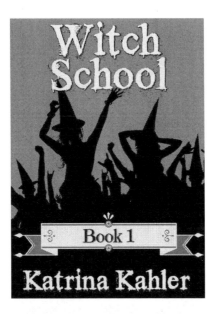

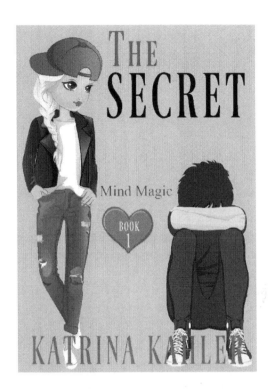

Made in the USA
Middletown, DE
12 December 2017